Superstar Kids

Rhyming moral fun!

Written by Gavin Rhodes
Illustrated by Aliyah Coreana

Published by New Generation Publishing in 2016

First Edition

ISBN: 978-1-78719-186-0

www.newgeneration-publishing.com

New Generation Publishing

Contents Page

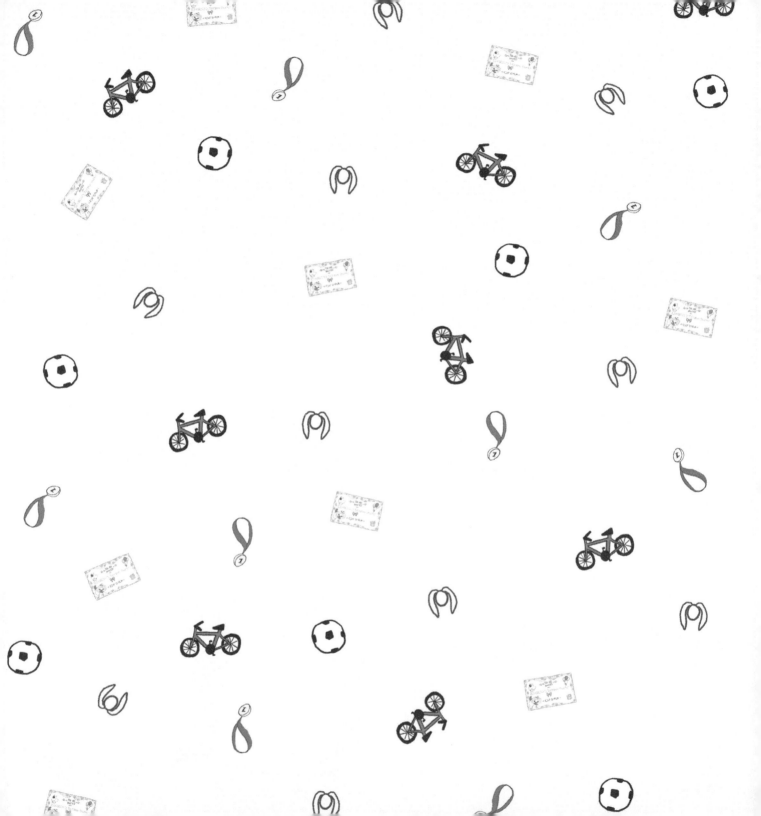

Bella & Bunny
"Tidy Your Room"

Bella loved her bunny; she cuddled him with PRIDE,
Wherever Bella went, bunny was by her SIDE.

From the toy shop he was new and FLUFFY,
But now little bunny was old and SCRUFFY.

Bella's room was always messy,
and though she didn't really MIND,
It meant her toys were hard to FIND.

One day she lost her
best friend, BUNNY,
This was no laughing
matter, it wasn't FUNNY.

Bella searched high and LOW,
Under the bed, in the toy box,
could she find him? - no, no, NO!

Two days went by and still bunny could not be FOUND,
She'd looked up and down and all AROUND.

Mummy even bought her a brand new one with shiny FUR
But this was just no good for HER.

'I want old bunny back,' Bella CRIED,

'Where on earth did bunny HIDE?!'

Mummy noticed
Bella's messy ROOM,
Her voice came out
with quite a BOOM...
'Your room is so
untidy please clear
everything AWAY'

'I don't want to,'
muttered Bella, 'not
TODAY!'

The next morning Bella woke
to a quiet rustling NOISE,
Bella sat up and listened, it was
coming from her pile of TOYS!

Rummaging through the toys,
Bella suddenly heard, 'Over here, it's ME!'
And to her amazement
there was bunny, squashed next to
Billy-bob bumble BEE.

Bella rubbed her eyes, 'I must be dreaming,' she SAID,
'You *are* dreaming!' announced bunny, 'you are still asleep in your BED!'

'Now remember... You must tidy your room every DAY,
Or you won't find your toys when you want to PLAY!'

Suddenly Bella woke, and ran to
the mountain of toys on the FLOOR,
Just like in her dream, she dived into the
pile and the search for bunny was no MORE.

Bella was so happy that bunny had RETURNED,
This certainly was an important lesson LEARNED!

Bella looked at bunny and said,
'You were right, losing you was too much STRESS!

'I will never again leave my room in a MESS!'

BRODY'S BOOTS

'Belief and Confidence'

Brody was completely soccer MAD, He always wore the boots
given to him by his DAD.

'Take good care of these boots,' his dad had said that DAY,
'They were lucky for me when I used to PLAY.'

The boots were blue and white with a flash of RED,
Brody's dad would say, 'I know you love them but
you can't wear them for BED!'

Soccer really was Brody's PASSION,
He would practise like it was going out of FASHION.

Striker was Brody's POSITION,
He scored lots of goals in every
COMPETITION.

Brody played for Milledge Rovers and he was the STAR.
In fact, he was the best player in the whole league by FAR.

He wore his lucky boots
for every GAME,
And felt proud when
the Rovers' fans
chanted his NAME.

Brody had helped his team
reach the final of the CUP,
And with his Dad's boots on
his feet he knew he'd lift
that trophy UP!

The big day arrived and Brody was READY,
But so was the Henwood Eagles' goalkeeper, Steady EDDIE!

'Oh no, my boots!
I've left them at home,'
Brody cried with a worried SHOUT.
"My lucky boots!
I can't play WITHOUT!'

It was time for
the kick off
and Brody was
in DESPAIR,
He had no
choice but to
wear his spare
PAIR.

Brody wasn't playing well at ALL,
In fact, he could hardly kick the BALL.

Half time and Rovers were losing one goal to ZERO,
Brody needed to become the HERO.

Ten minutes to go and for poor Brody's TEAM,
It seemed lifting the cup was to be nothing more than a DREAM.

Brody turned to
his dad,
his kit all MUCKY,
'I need my boots,
these old ones
aren't LUCKY'.

Dad replied, 'Don't worry about the boots, just believe in
yourself and try your BEST,'
'Now get back to it, there's no time to REST!'

Brody got the ball, dribbled past three and scored an absolute PEACH!
'What a goal' said Brody's dad, 'now that's one goal EACH.'

One minute left and Brody's tripped in the area; it's a penalty SHOT.
Brody steps up to the ball to give it all he's GOT.

He strikes the ball and the goalie goes the wrong WAY.
Rovers have won the cup, and Brody has saved the DAY.

Brody didn't need his lucky boots, his dad's words had made SENSE,
You should always believe in yourself and have a bit of CONFIDENCE!

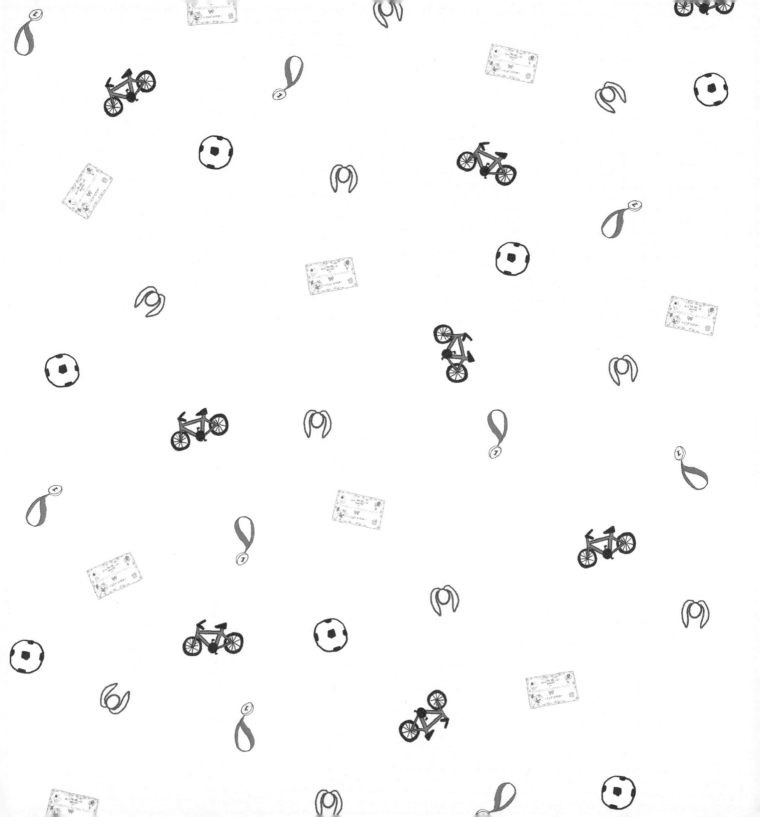

KIMBERLY'S PARTY!

'Kindness and Sharing'

Kimberly was so excited about her birthday
party she couldn't hide her JOY.
How many presents am I going to get? She thought,
which doll? Which dress? Which TOY?

Kimberly's mummy had arranged a big party, inviting MANY,
There would be balloons, games and a clown called KENNY.

Brooke was Kimberly's friend from school,
she lived on the other side of TOWN,
It was Brooke's birthday too but her parents
couldn't afford a party or a CLOWN.

Brooke's birthday was always quiet with
just her parents, grandma and brother KYLE,
She didn't mind but wished that one day she
could have a real party... Kimberly STYLE!

The day of Kimberly's party
was finally HERE,
Kimberly woke with a smile
but was not full of CHEER.

'What's the matter?' asked her
mummy with a surprised LOOK,
'I am excited about my party,' replied Kimberly,
'but I've been thinking about my friend BROOKE.'

'I so wanted her to COME,
But she's at home for her own
birthday with her dad and her MUM.'

'Spending your birthday with family is lovely of course...
but a party with friends is really FUN,
Especially on a day like this in the SUN.'

Later that day, Brooke heard some NOISE...
Music and laughter from happy girls and BOYS.

It was coming from the park over
the road, as far as she could TELL,
Then suddenly...
'ding-dong' went the DOORBELL.

She opened the door and there stood
Kimberly in her party dress with ribbons in her HAIR,
'Happy Birthday Brooke!' Take a look over THERE!'

Lots of children were gathered on the
green with gifts and BALLOONS,
There were tables full of food, a
big cake and party TUNES.

A sign with the words 'Brooke & Kimberly's
Joint Party' was hanging on a TREE,
Brooke looked at Kimberly and said,
'I can't believe you have done this for ME.'

The party was so much fun and a
great time was had by ALL,
Brooke was so happy, she had a BALL.

At bedtime, Kimberly's mummy said,
'I'm so proud that you're so thoughtful and CARING,
Remembering friendship is about kindness and SHARING.'

ELLIOT -and-

'Helping

Elliot was super SMART,
He was brilliant at all his subjects at school,
even cooking, drama and ART.

Elliot was top of the class for every TEST,
It all just came naturally, he was the BEST.

Felix on the other hand didn't
do so well at SCHOOL.
He was good at sport though,
especially swimming in the POOL.

Felix relished sports day as he
knew that he could WIN,
Exam day was a different story, test
scores would end up in the BIN.

One day after a maths test,
Felix was feeling DOWN.
'Don't worry Felix,' said Elliot,
'I can help you remove that FROWN.'

'You would help me?
Asked Felix in a surprised TONE,
'Yes sure,' replied Elliot,
whilst casually slurping ice cream from a CONE.

'How about, I help you with your study
and homework for a WHILE?
And you could teach me how to swim?'
suggested Elliot, with a cheeky SMILE.

'Swim?' Asked Felix with a puzzled look on his FACE,
'So, you can't swim?' He thought it was a DISGRACE!

'I can't swim very well, I want you to
help me swim like a SEAL!'
'Ok,' said Felix 'you have yourself a DEAL!'

The boys helped each other after school every DAY,
Making good progress and becoming friends along the WAY.

Felix quickly became more ABLE,
He finally got the hang of his times TABLE!

Elliot's swimming started to IMPROVE,
He gained confidence in the water and now he could really MOVE!

Sports day came and Elliot swam in his first RACE,
He didn't win but did so well, he finished in 2nd PLACE!

Felix had never been a maths WHIZZ,
But because Elliot had helped him,
he passed his latest QUIZ.

Helping each other was not a CHORE,
And it made a big difference
to the boys that's for SURE.

'It's good to help others in need,' Felix SAID.
Elliot agreed, nodding his HEAD.
'Let's see who else we can help,' Elliot CRIED,
Doing such a good deed filled him with PRIDE.

So, if you're at school,
or anywhere for that MATTER,
Try and help someone else,
or just be there if they want a NATTER.

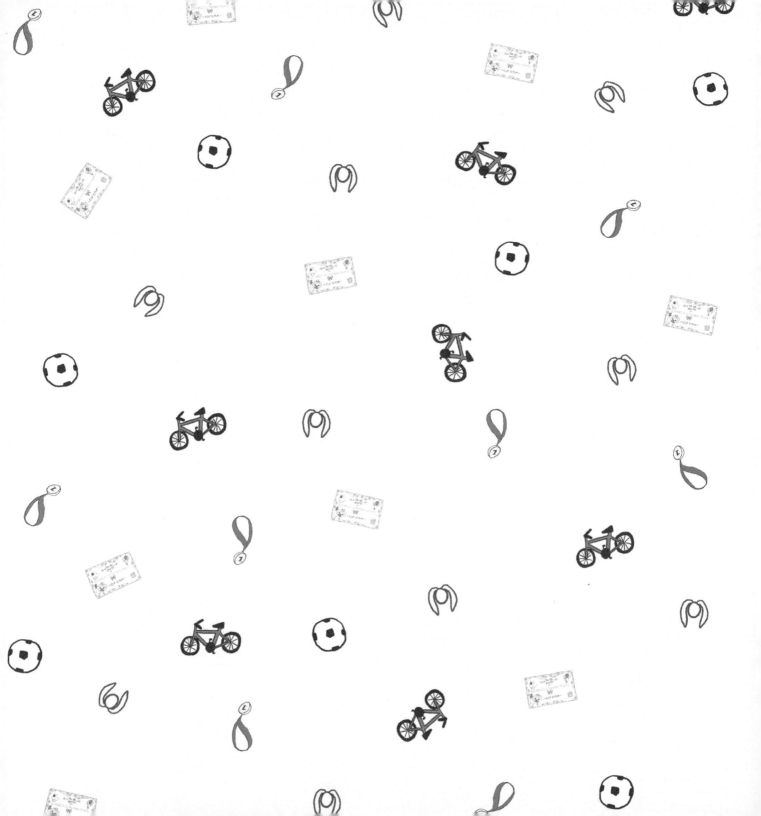

ROCO

'Behaving'

Roco was a very naughty six year OLD,
He was always up to mischief and never did as he was TOLD.

Some of his naughty antics INCLUDE...
Messing around in class and calling teachers 'DUDE';

Running around and shouting in SHOPS,
Whacking teddy with the cleaner's MOPS,

Hiding his sister's dollies in strange PLACES,
and drawing moustaches on their FACES.

Setting his sister's pet hamsters FREE,
Hanging like a monkey from the TREE,

Chasing the neighbour's CAT,
Writing 'NOT' on the welcome MAT,

Muddy footprints on the clean FLOOR,
Inky handprints on every DOOR,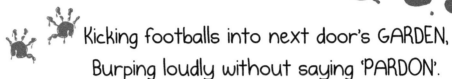

Kicking footballs into next door's GARDEN,
Burping loudly without saying 'PARDON'.

Turning on the sprinkler when everyone's on the LAWN,
Not putting his hand over his mouth for a YAWN.

Roco certainly was a cheeky little LAD,
He would often receive a telling off from his DAD.

One day Roco got in trouble at SCHOOL,
He got in a fight! It really was not COOL!

Roco's dad was very CROSS,
'You must behave and listen to me,'
he shouted, 'I'm the BOSS!'

'As a punishment you cannot ride your bike for a WEEK,
And no fun with your friends playing hide and SEEK.'

These were Roco's favourite things,
he loved to do them every DAY,
He really hated not going out to PLAY.

Roco watched his friends play outside from the window in his ROOM
His dad called up, 'Come and help with the chores, take this BROOM.'

Roco was starting to realise that being naughty wasn't all that FUNNY,
He didn't like doing chores and being stuck inside when it's SUNNY.

When the week was over Roco said, 'Dad,
I've made a plan to be good from now on,
well I will do my BEST!'
'Ok,' said dad, 'let's put it to the TEST!'

'If you are a good boy, for your birthday
I will buy you a new BIKE.'
'Wow,' said Roco, 'that idea I LIKE!'

Every little boy or girl should think
twice about being NAUGHTY,
Be smart, be good, maybe take up a
hobby or what about trying something SPORTY!

Lightning Source UK Ltd.
Milton Keynes UK
UKHW05f0843181018
330690UK00014B/96/P